Published by Hachette Partworks Ltd.
ISBN: 978-1-908648-92-1
Date of Printing: January 2017
Printed in Romania by Canale

Disney Princess

Cinderella

Disney

hachette

One day, Cinderella woke up, stretched and exclaimed, "What a lovely morning!" She smiled at the little songbirds who had come to wake her.

Since her father died, Cinderella had lived with her stepmother Lady Tremaine, and two stepsisters, Anastasia and Drizella.

Poor Cinderella was treated no better than a servant at home. She had to do all the housework and her sisters never lifted a finger to help.

One day, a royal messenger came to the house with a message from the King. All the young ladies in the kingdom were invited to a grand ball!

"Why, that means I can go too!" exclaimed Cinderella. Anastasia and Drizella laughed, but the Stepmother agreed Cinderella could go – if she finished her chores and found something suitable to wear.

In the attic, Cinderella found a dress that once belonged to her mother. It was a bit old fashioned, but Cinderella could fix it.

Then came a familiar cry from downstairs. “CINDERELLA!” The poor girl sighed. Her gown would have to wait until later.

Cinderella's stepsisters tossed armloads of clothes at her. Each one, they declared, needed mending and ironing at once. The Stepmother gave her even more chores.

Meanwhile, the mice and the birds searched in the Stepsisters' room and found some beads and ribbons.

With some clever stitching and folding, the animals soon turned Cinderella's simple dress into a fabulous ballgown!

At eight o'clock that evening, everyone was ready to leave for the ball – except poor Cinderella. Her stepfamily had made sure that she had no time to get ready.

Just then Cinderella saw her new dress.

"Surprise!" shouted the mice and birds.

"Oh, thank you so much!" Cinderella cried in delight.

When Anastasia and Drizella saw Cinderella, they flew into a jealous rage. They ripped the dress, pulling off the sash and yanking the beads, while the Stepmother just stood and watched.

Cinderella ran, heartbroken, into the garden.

Suddenly, someone appeared – it was Cinderella's fairy godmother! She declared that Cinderella would go to the ball. She waved her magic wand and turned a pumpkin into an elegant coach and the mice into fine horses.

Then the Fairy Godmother turned to Cinderella. In an instant, Cinderella was wearing a beautiful dress and sparkly glass slippers. The Fairy Godmother told Cinderella to be home before midnight when everything would change back.

At the palace, everyone was astounded by Cinderella's beauty. The Prince asked her to dance and they spent the whole evening together.

Suddenly, the clock began to chime midnight. Cinderella ran out of the castle, dropping one of her glass slippers on the staircase.

Cinderella reached the woods just as everything turned back to normal. All she had to remind her of her evening was a single glass slipper.

The next day, there was a royal proclamation. The Prince was searching for the girl who had dropped the glass slipper. He wanted to marry her!

The Grand Duke arrived with the glass slipper. Anastasia and Drizella rushed to prove it belonged to them, but neither one of them could squeeze their big feet into the dainty slipper.

Then the Stepmother tripped up the footman. The slipper shattered before Cinderella could try it on, but Cinderella still had the matching slipper in her pocket. It was a perfect fit!

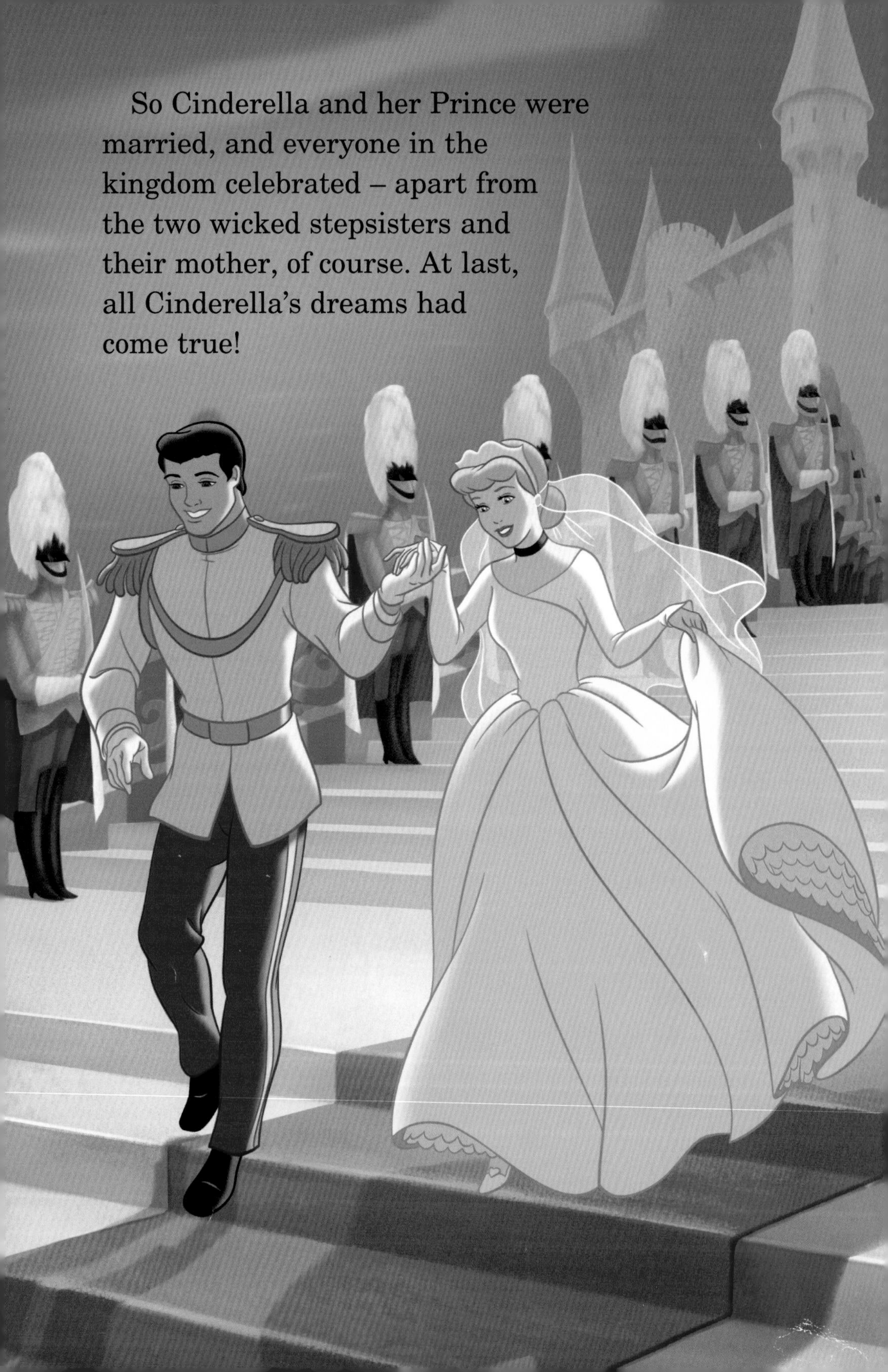

So Cinderella and her Prince were married, and everyone in the kingdom celebrated – apart from the two wicked stepsisters and their mother, of course. At last, all Cinderella's dreams had come true!